CW00866318

For Alex, wit

First published in 2023

ISBN   978-1-3999-7394-6

In a quiet little town, close to steep hills and green forests, there lived a curious boy named Alex. One day, eager for adventure he prepared his backpack with a water bottle, rope and a knife and began his usual hiking in the woods.

Alex had no idea that today would not be an average day. In fact, this would be the most remarkable day of his life.

Alex wandered through the forest in search of excitement, when he stumbled upon a colossal giant.
He stood frozen, while his heart was racing from fear and fascination. The giant moved with surprising grace but the ground was shaking after each step he took. Although the little boy was terrified, he decided to follow the giant and find out, where exactly is he going.

After awhile, the giant stopped in front of a huge cave. The walls surrounding it were engraved with ancient, mysterious symbols. The giant, with fingers as large as tree branches, pressed the symbols, revealing a secret passage deeper into the cave.
As the giant walked through this magical cave, Alex wondered if he was dreaming.

"How is this possible?"

"Giants don't exist!"

"He goes through a wall, with a glimmering mist?"

As the sun began to set, casting shadows across the forest, young Alex stood before the cave entrance.
He pressed the mysterious symbols, in the same order as the giant did, and then the pathway revealed itself.

For a moment, he hesitated, yet a drop of courage ran through his veins. Though his steps were cautious, his determination to uncover the secrets hidden within the cave pushed him to go further.

As he was walking, fear ran through him like a cold shower, urging him to go back from the unknown.

The sound of bats squeaking from the ceiling was echoing around Alex, but he couldn't go back, because he saw a light at the end of the cave.

He ran towards it, to escape the darkness and then he stood still in astonishment. His eyes were lying to him again, he thought.

"Wow, that's amazing!" gasped Alex in awe.

The view in front of him was breathtaking. Majestic mountains were touching the clouds. Green trees and wildflowers painted the landscape with the most beautiful colours he had ever seen. The blue streams through the magical valley were reflecting the sunset.
Alex stood stunned and amazed, feeling that he almost wasn't invited to see such an incredible place.

As he walked through the wonder valley, birds with enchanting melodies were singing around him. Even the air felt different. Alex continued ahead and saw a path that went up a hill.

"What is this place?" he asked himself out loud.

"Well, this is our home." said a voice up the hill.
Alex walked a little bit further and he saw two boys, but not just ordinary boys. They were giants, and they sounded friendly.

"Hello, my name is Alex, I come from the cave, uh... from my world. Who are You?"

"I am Tim and this is my brother Kai. I am ill, but we can still play tag if you want to?"

"Sure, but can you tell me Tim, why is your world hidden?" asked Alex.

"What my father told me was that, many years ago, the people from your world, had a war with us but we got tired of fighting. Then we decided

to hide in caves and secret passages around the world because we wanted peace. Since then, we thought that we were forgotten but..."
"Be quiet, Tim" a voice shook the grounds. Standing tall before them, was the giant from the cave.

"Our secrets are as old as the roots beneath us. Not everyone is worthy to know them.
Why are you here, boy?" demanded the giant.

"I...I... I followed you...I was just curious.." Alex trembled with fear.
"Curious? CURIOUS?" shouted the giant.
"Do you understand, that this land is sacred and no one should know about it? Only the worthy can stay!"

"I promise I won't tell..."

"SILENCE!" roared the giant.
"Here, we don't believe in words. You have to go, through the three challenges and then if you survive, you will be deemed worthy.
First, you will have to pass the crazy bridge, then the vicious volcano and finally the wild river and pick the apple of life."

Alex agreed, to honour the rules and found himself on a steep edge of a hill. In front of him, a long bridge, made of stones and ropes.

"This bridge is tricky. It will move, it will try to throw you off of it and only if you pass, it will become calm again" advised the giant.

The way down was long and it looked really dangerous, but Alex gained new powers within himself and started the obstacle.

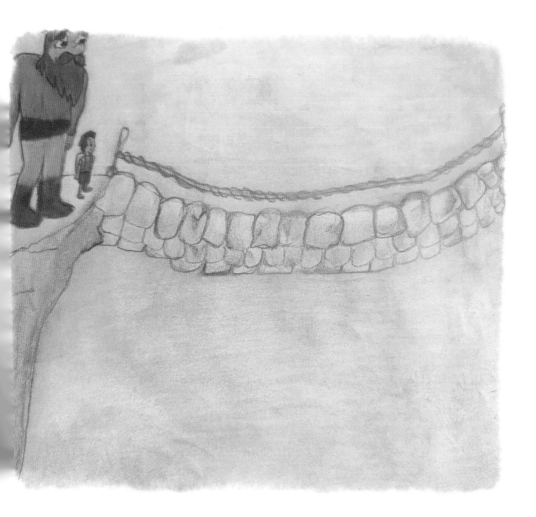

As soon as the boy stepped onto the bridge, he felt that the rocks become alive. The ropes started shaking left and right and Alex fell onto his knees grabbing the rocks with his fingers, squeezing them tightly. Then the ground swayed, tossing and turning Alex around.
The bridge was so angry, that someone dared to step on it, so with full force it started to tremble and shake while the little boy was thinking, how can he take another step forward.
Just then, Alex took out his knife and shoved it between two rocks while he caught the rope with the other hand. He moved slowly and cautiously, using all of his strength, while the bridge was making furious loops.

The last steps were the hardest and he almost gave up because his hands and legs were in excruciating pain.

"Come on boy, not long now" shouted the giant.

Alex took the last few steps and crashed into the ground, tired he fell asleep.

Later that night, when he woke up, his muscles were sore and he felt dizzy but the smell of delicious food was lingering around him. He stood up and went to the kitchen to see the giant, his wife, Tim and Kai. All of them were waiting for him and when they saw Alex, laughter and happiness filled the room.

"Sit down boy. You have to eat to be strong. You did well on the bridge, but more dangers await you." said the giant with a smile.

"I will do everything I can, to pass these challenges." said Alex with a grin.

"Don't be so proud boy. Every obstacle is more and more difficult than the previous one. We will see if you are lucky or you are worthy. The next challenge is very dangerous.

"You will have to climb to the top of the vicious volcano and if you succeed you can find and take the Emerald of Wisdom."

"The Emerald of Wisdom? What is that?" asked Alex. "It is a magical artefact, which shows the way when it's dark. You just point it to the stars and it will guide you like a compass. But only if you can get it."

Alex stayed long, watching the volcano and thinking about how to reach the top, avoiding the lava, when he had a great idea. There were a lot of rocks but he needed the perfect flat ones, which covered his feet.
The boy found a few and then took out his rope from the backpack. Then, he placed the rocks under his feet, tying them firmly around.

"This is a great idea" he thought, but when he started climbing the volcano, the lava became more and more closer to his feet. It was hot and the smoke that he was breathing, made him dizzy and he lost his balance.
He stepped on the boiling lava and one by one the ropes started burning under his feet.
Terrified, Alex jumped from the lava to a small space where he was safe.

He looked around, and trough the rivers of lava he saw a green sparkle.
There it was, this beautiful emerald, waiting to be found.
The boy was running out of time.
The ropes were burned and his feet exposed, so he took out his rope and tied them again.

He jumped over the lava rivers, to take the precious emerald, when
he finally reached it.
When he took it, it started glowing, showing the direction of the escape route.
Alex followed the green light when he saw a path which is free of lava, and he quickly came down from the volcano, running with pride towards the giant.

That night he couldn't sleep, knowing that the most dangerous challenge of all awaits him. The wild river. The giant told him that no man or animal had ever crossed this river alive.

The next day, they woke up early and went to face the last trial. The river looked extraordinary, filled with different shades of blue and purple.
"This is the last one. If you reach the end, grab the apple of life. It can cure any illness." said the giant.
As Alex dipped his toes into the cool water, he noticed a few piranhas ready to attack him.

He quickly took out his knife and stabbed the tail of one piranha. The wounded fish darted away, while the other piranhas started chasing it instead of the boy. Alex realised his chance so he quickly swam to safety.

Happy with the triumph over the piranhas, he
stepped on dry land where, before his eyes, a majestic
apple tree was revealed.
Alex carefully plucked one from the branch and put
it inside his pocket.
He wasn't prepared for what was about to come
when he went back to the wild waters.

As the young boy stepped into the river, the water felt uneasy. Hauntingly beautiful voices lingered around. Alex saw mesmerizing mermaids emerging from the water, singing the most beautiful melodies he had ever heard.

The unsuspecting boy listened with astonishment, not realizing, how he slowly was drifting to the dark depths of the river. He fell into a deep slumber, as the mermaids gathered around him, hoping he would drown.

As soon as he saw that, the giant shouted and shook the grounds
of the river with his thunderous voice. " Stand up boy!"
Alex woke up shaking and quickly scratched the mermaid's tail.
When the piranhas sensed the exposed flesh, they started chasing
the mermaid. When Alex came out of the river, the giant hugged
him and
said:

"You are now worthy, to stay in this world as it is yours, but you bear the responsibility of keeping the secret of this place. Never reveal it to anyone."

They went back to the giant's house and Tim was waiting outside.
"Tim, this is for you." said Alex while giving the apple of life.
"Are you sure? You can give it to anyone you choose." said Tim with tears in his eyes.
"You need it more than I do friend."
"Thank you, Alex. Now tell me everything about your adventure." Tim eagerly awaited.

Under the jungle's sunset, they spoke throughout the night, sharing tales of their adventures, dreams, and fears.
"What is your next quest?" asked Tim curiously.
"I haven't thought about that. I guess we shall see."
The giant watched them become best friends, grateful in his heart that the boy saved his son.